the THREE LITTLE PIGS
and the
Not So Big Bad Wolf

Library of Congress Control Number: 2024926059

Book Design – Sharon Kizziah-Holmes

SOLANDER
—PRESS—

Springdale Arkansas

Paperback ISBN 13: 978-1-959548-85-0
Hardback ISBN 13: 978-1-959548-84-3
eBook ISBN 13: 978-1-959548-86-7

the THREE LITTLE PIGS
and the
Not So Big Bad Wolf

by
Clarissa Willis

illustrated by
Nab Shaw

**A long time ago, three little pigs
built a home of bricks, straw, and twigs.**

One day, a big wolf came up to their door.
They had heard stories of that trick before.

"He wants to eat us," said Pig Number One.
Pig Two said, "Let's go see what he has done."

"Let's read what he wrote," suggested Pig Three.
"I'll read it out loud," Pig Two did agree.

"Forest-wide food drive tomorrow, all day.
Share what you can. We'll be coming your way."

"We've worked hard for that food," Pig Three cried.
"We are not sharing. Let's all go back inside."

That night, when the brothers went off to bed,
Pig Two did something much different instead.

He left most of their food outside by the gate.
It took quite a while, so he stayed up really late.

The very next morning, his brothers were mad.
Pig Three yelled "That's almost all that we had!"

"What in the world have you gone and done?
That's MY food!" screamed selfish Pig One.

**The two rushed outside to bring the food in.
Both froze in their tracks at what happened then—**

along came the wolf with a big black bear.
Pigs Two and Three were scared, standing there.

The pigs did not know what to say or to do.
Then, out of the house ran their brother, Pig Two.

"Hey, Wolf. Hey, Bear. Read your note on our wall.
That food by the gate is to share with you all."

"Thank you, Pig Two," Wolf said with a bow.
"We'll go and gather more food now.
There's a potluck tonight in the meadow at six.
Everyone's coming. It'll be quite a mix."

"We won't be there!" yelled pigs One and Three.
"You want to eat us. So go, leave us be."

"I'll make the soup," Pig Two noted with glee.
"I love a good party. You can count on me.
I'm sorry my brothers are so mean and crude.
I'm very displeased. They're just plain rude!"

Pig Two went inside in search of his brothers.
He tried to convince them to join the others.

"You're selfish pigs. You're just filled with fear.
I'm going to that party. I'm out of here."

Pig Two made the soup. He dressed up quite nice.
On the way to the party, he met three blind mice.

"Where are your brothers? There's a party, you know."
"My brothers, you see, are too selfish to go."

The three bears brought porridge.
The mice brought the cheese.
The rabbit made salad. Everyone was at ease.

Desserts were served
by the wolf and the bear.
Even Bo Peep's sheep were all there.

Wolf welcomed guests and then made his plea.
"I think it is time that we all agree,

this forest has hundreds of mouths to feed,
working together is what we do need."

"I propose we meet in the meadow, right here,
at six on Thursday each week of the year."

Behind a tree, pigs One and Three hid.
Everyone smiled when they saw what they did.

They walked to the wolf, and then they did say,

"The greed in our heart kept us away.
We've been very selfish, reluctant to share.
Your kind example has taught us to care."

Other Children's books by Clarissa

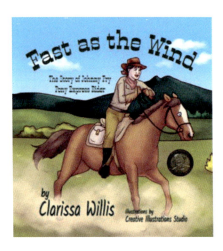

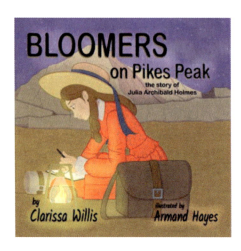

Johnny Fry was the first western rider for the Pony Express. From his humble beginnings in Missouri to his exciting first ride in 1860, Johnny never gave up. Even though he was small for his age, his love for horses helped him become one of the true heroes of the American west. With practice and determination, Johnny learned to ride like the wind.

Julia Archibald Holmes was not one to back down from a challenge, especially when it meant fighting for justice. Her journey to the top of Pikes Peak was just the beginning of her many adventures. In the mid-1800s, amidst the rugged terrain of the Rocky Mountains, Julia Archibald Holmes set out to make a name for herself. Her life was a series of daring escapades, all in the name of justice. Her involvement in the Underground Railroad, a perilous journey fraught with risk, was a testament to her unwavering commitment. Her later advocacy for Women's voting rights was a continuation of this fearless spirit.

However, as Julia's diary reveals, her journey was not without its challenges. From facing dangerous obstacles to overcoming personal setbacks, her unwavering commitment to justice would be tested. Julia's story provides a powerful message of determination, courage, and resilience that will leave a lasting impact on readers.

About the Author

Clarissa (Chrissy) Willis is the product of a minister and a drama teacher. She has always had an active imagination and enjoys speaking and writing. She's lived in nine states. She was a major corporation's senior vice president of publishing and has been an educator for over 40 years. As a child growing up in Little Rock, Arkansas, she wrote stories and got into trouble for a variety of mishaps, from the attempted murder of her brother, a crime she swears wasn't her fault, to robbing the collection plate at church.

She earned a PhD in Early Childhood Special Education from the University of Southern Mississippi. In her professional life, Dr. Willis has provided workshops and keynote addresses in all 50 states and three foreign countries. She is a professor emeritus from the University of Sothern Indiana. Clarissa has written curricula for Frog Street Press, Kaplan Early Learning Company, and Scholastic. She has authored nineteen teacher resource books, including the award-winning Teaching Young Children with Autism Spectrum Disorder. In addition, she has written four children's books and is working on a memoir.

In her spare time, she serves on the board for Ozark Creative Writers, Between the Pages Writers Conference, and the Missouri Writers' Guild. She lives with her dogs, George and Gracie, in the Ozark Mountains of Northwest Arkansas. You can contact her at clarissa@clarissawillis.com.

About the Illustrator

Nab Shaw is a seasoned graphic designer with a diverse range of design expertise. His passion lies in transforming ideas into visual narratives, a skill he has honed over his 6.5 years in the industry. His proficiency spans various design disciplines, including branding, digital illustration, print design, and web graphics. This breadth of experience allows him to create comprehensive and cohesive visual identities for a wide array of clients and projects, instilling confidence in his ability to handle any design challenge.

His expertise is showcased in a diverse portfolio that includes children's book illustrations, such as whimsical and fantasy art, cartoon-style kids' art, animal characters, fairytale illustrations, nursery rhyme art, educational art, digital and hand-drawn art, and watercolor kids' art. He has also designed retro vintage posters for films, movies, and music albums, capturing the essence of punk band and skateboard culture, leaving a lasting impression on his audience.

Additionally, he created travel posters, adventure story illustrations, oracle cards, playing cards, tarot cards, and vintage children's art. He designed book covers and illustrations for children's picture books on Amazon Kindle and Amazon KDP.

Made in the USA
Monee, IL
07 February 2025

11864534R00026